Opening Day Collection

FRIENDS OF THE DAVIS PUBLIC LIBRARY

7,000 New Books

First published in the United States, Great Britain, Canada, Australia, and New Zealand in 1999
by North-South Books Inc., an imprint of NordSüd Verlag AG, CH-8005 Zürich, Switzerland.
Revised and reillustrated edition published in 2010.
Distributed in the United States by North-South Books Inc., New York 10001.

Library of Congress Cataloging-in-Publication Data is available.
ISBN: 978-0-7358-2292-4 (trade edition)
Printed in Belgium by Proost N.V., B 2300 Turnhout, November 2009.
1 3 5 7 9 • 10 8 6 4 2

www.northsouth.com

FSC
Mixed Sources
Product group from well-managed
forests and other controlled sources
Cert no. BV-COC-070303
www.fsc.org
© 1996 Forest Stewardship Council

The Little Green Goose

by Adele Sansone

illustrated by Anke Faust

NorthSouth
New York / London

In a cozy barn on a cozy farm there lived four hens, a noisy rooster, a cluster of chicks, Daisy the farm dog, and Mr. Goose. Mr. Goose loved to play tag or hide-and-seek with the young chicks, and he often took them for a swim or read them a story.

But Mr. Goose wasn't happy, for he had a secret wish. He longed for a chick of his own, a baby that he could raise himself. A downy little goose who would call him Daddy.

"I'm going to make my dream come true," Mr. Goose decided, and he went to see the brown hen.

"Good day, Mrs. Brownhen," he said politely. "Would you be kind enough to give me one of your fine eggs? I would so much like to raise a baby chick."

"CLUCK?" Mrs. Brownhen was so startled that she almost fell out of her nest. "You're not a hen—you're a goose!" she said.

Poor Mr. Goose waddled away sadly.

That night he thought it over. There was nothing wrong with wanting to be a father. And if he had no wife to lay him an egg, he had no choice but to ask the hens. So back he went, this time to Mrs. Whitehen, Mrs. Blackhen, and Mrs. Speckledhen.

"Good day, dear hens," he said. "Would any of you be kind enough to give me one of your eggs? I would like to raise a baby chick myself."

"CLUCK, CLUCK, CLUUUUUCK!"
The hens were outraged.

Once again, Mr. Goose waddled sadly away.

Daisy found him sitting glumly on a rock.

"WOOF, WOOF!" she barked excitedly. "I heard you want an egg. Come with me. I think I can help."

Daisy led the way to a corner of the field at the edge of the woods.

There on the ground
was an egg.
A GIANT egg.

"I found it! I dug a hole for my bone, and I found this egg!" said
Daisy. "It's a bit old and smelly, but maybe you can still hatch it."
"Oh, thank you! Thank you!" said Mr. Goose.

Mr. Goose quickly built a nest, climbed up onto the egg, and waited.
Day after day he sat there, dreaming of his baby goose.

One morning, Mr. Goose heard a soft tap, and a tiny crack appeared in the egg. The crack grew bigger and bigger until a teeny little beak started to poke out. Or was it a beak?

Suddenly there was a loud CRACK, and a chick emerged.

It was bright green! It had beautiful shiny scales. It had a long tail too.

The chick stared at Mr. Goose. Mr. Goose stared at the chick.

"Mommy?" peeped the chick.

"Er, Daddy," said Mr. Goose.

"Daddy!" cried the chick.

"Here he is! Here he is!" cried Mr. Goose. "He called me Daddy!"

Daisy ran around barking. She had never seen a goose like this.

"Isn't my baby beautiful?" said Mr. Goose.

"Indeed he is," said Daisy. "He is a beautiful green goose."

"Daddy!" peeped the little green goose. "Hungry!"

Mr. Goose fed his baby worms and snails and other yummy things. Every night, he gabbled a bedtime story. And then, right before his baby fell asleep, he said, "Close your eyes and sleep under my wing, for you are my little green goose and I love you."

The little green goose grew and grew.

One morning, Mr. Goose said, "Now, my son, I think you're big enough to meet the other animals."

Mr. Goose was proud of his son. He was sure the others would be amazed. And how amazed they were! Mr. Goose had actually hatched a chick. And what a chick! They had never seen anything like it!

A few weeks later, the little green goose
was walking around the farmyard by himself.
He could hear the chicks chatter and the hens
giggle when he walked past.

"I'm very sorry to say it," said the rooster,
"but you are not a proper goose."

"Yes, I am," said the little green goose. "Mr. Goose is my daddy."

"No, you're not," said the rooster. "Take a look at yourself. You don't have feathers. You don't have a beak. And you're green! Mr. Goose cannot possibly be your daddy."

The little green goose began to cry. He ran to the pond and looked in the water. The rooster was right. He didn't have feathers or a beak, and he was green. He didn't look one bit like a goose.

"I'm going to find my real daddy," he decided.

On a stone by the bank sat a fat green frog.

"You are as green as I am!" cried the little green goose happily. "You must be my daddy!"

"Ribbit," said the frog. "No. I'm sorry. I'm not." And he leaped away.

"He's not my daddy," said the little green goose.

Just then a fish with bright green scales swam past.

"Are you my daddy?" the little green goose called out.

"Blup, blup," said the fish. "It's none of my business." And he swam away.

"He's not my daddy either," said the little green goose.

But then he saw a green lizard with glistening green skin and a long tail.

"You look just like me! You must be my real daddy!"

"Sssssss," said the lizard. "I'm not!"

"Yes, you are!"

"I am not!" said the lizard. "I've never seen an animal like you."

"But I am here!" cried the little green goose. "I must look like somebody! Who is my real daddy?"

"It is certainly not me," said the lizard.

The little green goose sat down and cried. "I'm just a baby! I need a daddy!"

He was hungry. Who would give him something to eat?

He was tired. Who would make him a soft nest?

But most of all, the little green goose was lonely. Who would love him?

Suddenly he leaped to his feet and began to run.

He ran past the lizard with the long green tail.
He ran past the fish with the bright green scales.

He ran past the frog, who was sitting on his stone again.

He ran faster and faster.
Now he knew who his daddy was.
"Daddy! Daddy!" he called.

"It's about time you came home for supper," said Mr. Goose fondly. "I've been looking for you."

"Daddy!" said the little green goose. And he snuggled his head happily under his father's warm wings.